Broken Promise

C.H. James

Golden Storm Publishing

Broken Promise – Curvy Girl Getaway Series – Book One

Paperback - First Edition

Cover designed by Golden Storm Publishing

Join the
C.H. James
ommunity!

Steamy Story. Happily Ever After. Hot Heroes.

GIVEAWAYS. FREE BOOKS.
WEEKLY NEW RELEASES.

Make sure you don't miss out on any of my new releases by signing up for my newsletter.
SIGN UP TO MY NEWSLETTER at https://bit.ly/chjamesnewsletter.

C.H. James
xoxo

Blurb

A weekend getaway, filled with curvy steam, changes every-thing for this English footballer.

James Hawkes

Being Britain's newest football hero has its perks.
By most people's standards, I'm living the high life. I get paid to play the game that I love. Not only that, but it's for one of the best soccer clubs in London; the best city in the world.
But when I decide to take a weekend break to get some time to myself, never did I expect my sister's plus-sized best friend to be shacking up at my luxurious beachside apartment. Victoria's luscious curves had always done things to me that I couldn't explain, but I'd sworn off her years ago, promising my sister I'd never go there.
I can't bear to see her so down in the dumps, and I make it my mission to make her believe she's desirable, even to England's favorite footballer.
One kiss is all it takes, and one steamy night later, everything has changed. Now I have to face my sister and put it all on the line for love.

Curvy Girl Getaway Series is a collection of instalove novellas filled with strong girls, HEA & the sexiest book boyfriends. Each book in the series is a standalone and they can be read in any order.

Chapter One

Victoria

A CLATTERING OF PLATES makes the hair on my neck prickle and the tongs I had been swinging on my finger drop to the floor.

"Shit," Sophie mumbles, eyeballing Grant, Head Chef and my asshole boss from beneath the serving bay. "Is he ever in a good mood?"

I shake my head. "Nope."

"Bugger. No wonder you want to get away this weekend…"

Sophie leans her shoulder against the wall and looks out across the dining room, tucking a few stray strands of her straightened dark hair behind her ear. She looks amazing, as always. She had been making a habit of dropping in to see me before heading out for a night of dancing and random hook ups and one-night stands. By now, she'd given up on begging me to join her. The last thing I felt like doing after I hung up my chef's apron at the restaurant, *Le Rêver,* where I work seventy hours a week, was to spend the next four hours dancing with myself as everyone on the dancefloor avoided the large curvy girls and instead dragged the skinny girls dancing beside us away to feel them up in a dark corner instead.

But I don't hold it against Sophie. She's beautiful. Curvy like me, only bustier. She has good genes because everyone in her family is gorgeous… lucky bitch.

The Hawkes family are well off. They always have been and now that Sophie's brother, James, is England's star striker on the football pitch, their fame is growing as quickly as their bank accounts.

My stomach tightens at the thought of James Hawkes and the garnish of parsley I toss over the steaming steak makes a mess of Grant's perfectly laid out vegetable medley.

"Seriously though," Sophie says as she continues to distract me, despite watching me glance over my shoulder, hoping Grant hasn't seen the mess I've made of his perfectly cooked dish. "Why do you want to leave London on Valentine's Day weekend? Remind me again, when was the last time you were shagged?"

Sophie pins me with a pointed look and her eyes remind me of her twin brother. The brother I had sworn off many years ago, just as she had with mine. We decided when we were fourteen that our friendship was the best friendship planet Earth had ever had the pleasure of witnessing. We were the funniest duo in history. No contest.

So brothers were ruled out-of-bounds.

Not that Sophie had to worry about James ever taking a fancy in me. As far as I was concerned, I was invisible to him. Harry, my brother, on the other hand, had always taken a liking to brunettes and Sophie had ignored more than a few advances on his behalf over the years.

"It hasn't been that long…" I shy away, avoiding Sophie's wide eyes.

"How long?" Sophie's fist firms and I know that my best friend won't drop it.

"Soph… Fuck…" A young waiter squeezes behind me and I suck in to allow him to pass. The young guys hips grind against my ass as he brushes past and Sophie flashes her brows at me from over the counter. "Yes, that is the most action I've had in a couple of years."

"Years?" Sophie chokes and I stare her down, warning her to lower her voice. "You're staying in London. Come out with me. Tonight."

"VICTORIA!" Grant's deep voice startles me from behind and I turn quickly to see his face a brighter red than usual. "IF I HAVE TO TELL YOUR STUPID BIMBO BITCH FRIEND TO FUCK OFF ONE MORE TIME, YOU'RE FIRED. NOW READ OUT THAT ORDER!"

I pull the receipt from the order machine and look at Sophie through the top of my eyes, the pain of having to listen to my Head Chef's abusive taunts for the rest of the night making them water.

"I need to get away. I need a break. I'm sorry. Maybe next weekend." I whisper quickly, pretending to read the receipt before announcing the new order to the kitchen. "Now get out of here before I lose my job."

When I look up, I see Sophie bursting through the exit of the restaurant, her tight dress hugging her figure. Despite her curves, she owns it. She always did. My stomach sinks, she will have the choice out of a line of guys at the club tonight, I'm sure of it.

And me? I'm stuck here. A deep sigh leaves my chest and I suck in a big breath, put on my big girl pants and read out the new orders with a bellowing voice.

"One Valentine's Special, one with mustard sauce and one with pepper gravy," I yell loudly as Grant glares at me while pulling out two fresh steaks and slaps them down on the grill.

I turn back to the serving bench and garnish two decedent heart-shaped mud cakes with a dolloping of cream and slam my fist on the bell to get the waiters attention. I watch him stalk over, collect the two plates in one hand and prance over to a table where a young couple smile at him, then to each other.

My lips lift with a smile as the fair-haired guest scoops a spoonful of his cake and holds it out for his partner to lean over and devour. Before realizing exactly what the hell I was doing, my tongue swipes over my lips, in unison with the gorgeous blonde's tongue as she flashes her tongue in the same way, battering her lashes at her Valentine's date.

I'm going to be alone forever.

★★★

My eyes burn in the freezing wind as it whips across the station platform. Winter is nearing an end, and it can't come quick enough. Nor could Sophie, who was supposed to meet me here to give me the keys to their family's beachside condo before the train drags me away from the hustle and bustle of a London weekend.

I pull out my phone and begin typing a message before a tap on my shoulder startles me.

"Shit!" My phone drops to the ground and I wince at the sound of the shattering screen.

"Sorry, babe!" Sophie's large blue eyes flash at me. She bends down to retrieve my now useless phone. "Bloody hell, you're on edge. You really do need this weekend getaway, don't you?"

Sophie dangles a set of keys in front of my face and my eyes light up. The passengers on the landing around me begin to move towards the yellow line, suitcases towing behind them. The ground vibrates, and Sophie had made it just in time.

"Oh, thank you so much," I gasp, clutching the keys. "And you're sure no one will be there?"

Images of me stumbling through the door clutching to bags of steaming hot takeaway and the biggest bottle of red wine that I could find flash before my eyes. Only in my head, James was there with his posse of gorgeous models, all falling at his magical feet which were renowned around England for whipping in dead-accurate spot kicks.

I gulp down and squash the anxious nerves rising up my throat.

"I'm sure. My parents are in Barcelona, half your luck. And James? I'm sure he's busy with training and everything else that goes along with being the new Golden Boy of the Three Lions."

Sophie assures me with a firm grasp of my shoulder, her dark hair flowing in the freezing wind. She lowers her gaze to me and gives me one final look as the train pulls into the platform with a deafening shriek.

"Are you sure you don't want me to come? I got mine last night, you know…" Sophie says.

She winks and her tongue pokes around on the inside of her cheek over and over, as if something long, hard and grand was pushing inside her mouth. I get the gesture. Except, I didn't *get* any of it.

"I'll be fine," I reply, slapping Sophie who was now doing the hand movements to match her tongue. "This is my Valentine's weekend."

I appreciate Sophie's offer. I do. It wasn't the first time she had been willing to throw everything away to come to my rescue. She would literally drop everything just to come and watch the latest installment of *Outlander* with me. No questions asked.

She's just that kind of friend.

But not anymore.

I'm tired of relying on her to pick me up every time my life seemed like I was destined to end up alone.

I didn't need a man to be happy. Just give me a decent Spanish Tempranillo and Netflix… Maybe throw in the luxurious tub at the beachside apartment, and that to me, was heaven. I was Willy-fucking-Wonka in his factory.

"I've gotta go," I say, pulling the handle on my case up. "I'll text-"

Sophie peers down at the smashed phone in my hand and her brows shoot up.

"Nevermind," I say, rolling my eyes. "I'll talk to you when I get back then!"

The train ride is quick. London to Brighton and Hove only takes an hour, and even with the weird wirey-grey haired man staring at my thick thighs the entire journey, the journey was quick. I gather my case and exit the station as quickly as possible, doing my best to lose the tail of the weird man.

I know the way to the apartment having accompanied Sophie on many family trips over the years. However, the pouring rain was making it difficult to see more than five meters in front of me, and the wind had picked up since I left London. The traffic's gone ballistic in the wild weather. The horns and emergency service sirens were echoing with an ear-splitting screech along the main strip of the beachside town and I can't move fast enough to escape the downpour.

Brighton and Hove is a nice seaside town, the closest to London by train. It's close enough to escape for a night, but far enough away to escape the hustled streets of London. On a fine day, the blue sky in Brighton is the perfect backdrop to the Brighton Pier where Sophie and I had spent hours with James, throwing our money away on the rides and side show attractions.

Now that I was older, all I wanted to do was pull up a deck chair on the pebbled beach, pull down my overly large sunglasses and slurp down as many tequila sunrises as possible.

I squint out at the horizon and shield my eyes from the rain. Dark clouds sprawl as far as I can see and there's no sign of the rain stopping.

Fat chance of seeing any kind of sunrise this weekend.

Finally, with my dripping wet clothes clinging to every bump and curve of my drenched body, I stumble up the stairs to the Hawkes' family getaway. With the image of the steaming tub quickening my movements, I dive in my bag and retrieve the keys Sophie delivered and turn the lock.

No click.

Hmmm…

With the key still in the door, I grip the knob and twist. Rain splatters on my back and a wild gust of wind makes the droplets smash against my cheek with a painful splash. The door swings open and the sound of hard rock music blaring down the entrance hallway instantly sends my stomach sinking back down to the bottom of the stairs.

James.

Chapter Two

James

"Bro, someone's here," I poke my head around the corner and see my sister's best friend, Victoria, lugging a suitcase in through the front door. She's dripping wet and my throat feels like it has closed over. Her clothes are gripping her stunning body and I swallow down hard. "I've gotta go."

"Come back to London!" Gary McShane, my teammate, yells out from the other end of the phone before I'm able to hammer my finger down on the button to swiftly end the call.

Shit. What the hell is she doing here?

Panic runs through my body, and I begin to pace back and forth in the kitchen. I wait for my sister's voice to echo up the hallway, but it never comes. I turn the music down, hoping that it had just drowned out Sophie's squeaky, childish voice.

"Hello?" Victoria calls out, her voice hunting me down.

"Victoria?" I reply, my voice breaking like it did whenever Victoria spent the night at our place all those years ago when we were both teenagers.

Within seconds I had gone from deflecting Gary's persistent nagging about catching the next train back up to London to join him on, and I quote, '*the best night of the year to pick up horny, needy, single chicks!*' to choking on my own words.

Gary is one of the youngest players on the team and the enjoyment of using his newly found fame for raking in 'hot chicks' was wearing thin. It had been three weekends in a row now, all hours that we weren't on the training pitch or sleeping had been spent trawling the clubs of Soho in search of the perfect girl – or two – to spend the night with.

And with Valentine's Day being this weekend, Gary was out to complete the quadruple.

Hence my escape to my family getaway in Brighton. Gary knew I didn't let my teammates stay here. It was a family place. Not a place for partying with the lads. What he didn't know was that I was just trying to get away from him so I didn't have to pretend that yes, I did pick up a 'hottie', and yes, I did fuck her like the 'maddog' she was.

I didn't do any of those things, by the way.

I just said that so Gary kept quiet for a few minutes after smashing a congratulatory high five on my palm.

"James?" Victoria's voice sings up the hallway again and my stomach does a flip.

I poke my head out of the door and it's a double flip for my insides.

"What are you doing here?" I step out, doing my best to control my eyes as they search up and down Victoria's body.

Cut it out. She's Sophie's best friend. She's off-limits.

"Soph said I could use the apartment for the weekend," Victoria says, dropping her handbag to the floor. "I – I hope that's OK. I can go if you have plans…"

Take her bag you wanker. What's wrong with you?

Shaking my head, I jump into gear and step over to relieve her of her suitcase.

"No, no, not at all!" I say, perhaps too enthusiastically. "I didn't tell anyone I was going to be here. I was trying to-"

"Escape?"

Victoria cuts me off, finishing my sentence for me and her lips pull into the stunning smile that, until this moment, I hadn't realised that I missed so much. Her red lipstick is glowing, her long, wavy red hair flowing down ever so elegantly. Despite being drenched from the bouncing rain outside, Victoria was every bit as beautiful as I remembered.

"Yeah," I say softly. "Escape."

There was a moments silence before Victoria shuffled on her feet. "It must be hard, being a famous footballer and all now…"

I shrug and look down at my feet. The last time I saw Victoria, I was still just an academy player. I might have made one or two senior appearances for my football club, Hampstead F.C., but I wasn't the star that I am now. I glance up and her eyes study me… Those big, gorgeous green eyes that I had dreamed about for so long.

"So you're alone?" Victoria looks over my shoulder, her brows raised in a way that make me think she's surprised.

Being a famous football player in London has its perks, of course it does. And footballers in England have a reputation for playing the field. See Gary McShane for example. But I hadn't ever bought into the whole casual sex embargo like my teammates had. I couldn't bring myself to do it, not when I had feelings for – never mind. I won't go there, especially not right now.

For years, I had been wearing the brunt of all the jokes in the locker room. Even my manager had asked me to give him the heads up when I decide to come out of the closet, so he had enough time to prepare for the media coverage that would no doubt send waves through the mainstream sports news. Imagine the frenzy: *England's Golden Boy Finally Comes Out.*

They'd have to reinforce the gates at Hampstead FC so they held the crowd of frantic media out.

"Yeah, I'm alone," I look around, as if searching for someone, too. "Why? You surprised?"

Victoria shrugs her shoulders and with it, my pride is shattered.

"You're famous now, Jimmy," Victoria says.

"Jimmy?" My chest pushes out and my heart leaps. "It's been years since anyone called me that. You're the only one, you know?"

It was Victoria's turn to look at her feet, but not before I could see the blush redden her soft cheeks. My heart is racing, and I can't remove my eyes from Victoria. Her feet are twisting on the dark wooden floorboards, her clothes dripping wet.

I take her in like she's been the thing missing from my life. A life so full of fame, money and fandom.

But suddenly, in the presence of Victoria, all of that felt… Irrelevant.

"How about a shower then?" I say, lifting the suitcase with one arm and turning to begin the ascend upstairs.

"What?" Victoria spits, her eyes wide. I turn and she's standing there, looking at me like a deer in headlights, her breathing panicked.

"A shower…" I say again, taking yet another second longer to realise why Victoria was so panicked. "You! You shower! Not me! Shit!"

I drop the suitcase to the floor and one of the wheels catches my toe, sending a shooting pain up my leg. Victoria rips her coat off, throws it to the floor and guides me to the kitchen where she pulls a chair from the table and lowers me down.

"I'm *so* sorry," Victoria says. She's crouching down with my bare foot wrapped in her freezing cold hands.

"It's fine," I groan. "Seriously, my fault. My fault entirely."

"Oh god… The whole of England will hate me now. I've injured James Hawkes. *The Hawk.* The best in a generation. Oh, shit… Oh, God!" Victoria shoots up from the floor and begins pacing in exactly the same spot I had been when she burst through the front door minutes ago.

"Seriously," I stand up and move over to hold her by the shoulders, anchoring her to one spot. I pin her down and her chest is rising rapidly. "I'm fine. It just hit a nerve."

I find myself breathing her in and silence grips the kitchen. My hands are firmly clasped to Victoria's shoulders, and I don't want to move. Her scent draws me in… Her eyes linger on my lips for a second, and then up to my eyes. My hands feel like they're burning and the energy between our bodies is almost too much.

The discarded coat has left Victoria in a tight tank top, which was probably white when she left London. Now, the water-logged coat had soaked through, and I could see a bright pink bra strap under the see-through fabric beneath my fingers.

I feel like we've been standing here all weekend. Time no longer exists – nor does it matter. All that matters right now, is…

"Victoria?" I choke, my throat once again doing its best to suffocate the words trying to leave my body. "You're standing on my toe."

"Fuck!" Victoria bounces off my toe and speeds through the doorway, her dripping clothes leaving a trail through the kitchen.

★★★

After ensuring Victoria that my right foot would be fine, and if it wasn't, the football clubs insurance would pay for any surgery required (she didn't find this the least bit funny), we settle in the sitting room for a warm cup of tea.

Rain streamed down the window, blurring the normally amazing view of the pier and the beach below. The room feels dark, despite the fact that we haven't even eaten lunch yet.

"You're still at that place?" I splutter, amazed that someone could put up with the infamous yelling chef at *Le Rêver's*. "You need a fucking medal or something."

"He's not that bad," Victoria says, almost spitting her tea out when I raise my brows across at her.

I had been doing my best not to stare ever since she descended the stairs after her shower, which, for the record, I had politely gathered a towel and closed the door after showing the way, climbing down the stairs with only an imaginary image of her full bust in my mind.

But as she covered her giggle with a shy hand, I couldn't pull my eyes from her. The see through tank top had been replaced with a low cut top, which now showed off so much of her cleavage, that I was sure I could see the darkening of her areoles. The air in the room must have been cool, too, because her nipples were definitely stiffened, and they poked through the cotton on her top like a warning signal.

'*WARNING: YOU CAN LOOK, BUT YOU CAN'T TOUCH.*'

I certainly didn't feel the crispness of the air, and the tightness in my pants had only just settled down after watching her walk in the room. I made a mental note to avoid sports trousers for as long as Victoria was here. If she was going to prance around in comfy yoga pants for the entire weekend, jeans were my go-to. I had no choice. Denim would provide more assistance in hiding my bulging crotch whenever her firm ass cheeks wobbled right before my eyes.

"So why is a budding bachelorette hiding away from London on Valentine's Day?" I ask, probing. Her eyes widen and look at me. "Not that it's any of my business…"

"It's fine. I just needed to get away… Work is hectic. My room-mates are driving me bonkers. Plus, I didn't have a date anyway. I've sort of given up after the last few creeps that I've been out with…" Victoria says, reaching across to the coffee table and collecting one of my favorite Scottish shortbread biscuits. She takes a bite, and I can almost feel the crumbly texture melting in her mouth. She sinks in the chair, holding the biscuit out before her gaping eyes. She looks to me, alive with pleasure and we nod knowingly at each other. "Oh, this shortbread is amazing!"

"Only the best here, baby!" I say, loud and proud. Victoria throws the rest of the biscuit in her mouth and I watch her tongue swipe across her lips. *Oh god.* "Um, so… What's been wrong with the last few blokes?"

"Well, there was the one who insisted that I only order a sal-ad…"

"What?! Prick!"

"Oh, it gets better," Victoria waves me down, insisting that I bottle my rage until she's finished. "Let's see… Oh yeah! Then there was the doctor. He started out OK, but as the night ran longer and we got to dessert, he started dropping hints about lap bands…"

My ears begin to burn. How dare anyone say these things to any human being, let alone Victoria.

"Where are these guys? I'll go around and sort them out," I growl, dodging Victoria's waving hands.

"Not necessary," Victoria says, collecting another shortbread and passing one to me too. "And then there was a dreamy Spanish traveller who I got along really well with… Until he pulled me into a dark alley and tried to snatch my bag and run."

My mouth drops and a deep gasp expands my lungs. "I hope you went to the station…"

"Oh, I didn't need to," Victoria smiles, her white teeth glowing and bringing life to the dull, dark and dreary day. "He didn't get far."

"That's my girl. Don't worry about those bell ends. They wouldn't be able to see beauty if it smacked them in the crotch." I pat Victoria's leg and after a few seconds, I realised my hand remains resting there. Heat prickles the palm of my hand, and yet again my sports pants are being tested. But I don't want to let go. "It's nice to see you anyway. It's been years, right? And hey, you're free to come down here whenever you want, OK?"

My stomach flutters at the sight of Victoria's lifting smile, and I gulp down the buttery crumbs that suddenly feel so dry in my throat.

"Thanks," Victoria says, her voice soft and sweet. "I love it here."

"Well, what's mine is yours," I say.

And I now pronounce you husband and wife.

Oh shit.

Chapter Three

Victoria

WE EAT LUNCH TOGETHER, reminiscing about weekends spent here when we were younger. We laugh at the stories of Sophie and me running up and down the stairs, spying on James while he watched the 3 o'clock kick-off on television. Sophie would throw things at him and, even though I thought he was well fit, even back then, I joined in the torment.

Eventually, I trot upstairs to have a lay down and I start doing that thing where I panic for absolutely no reason. James ducked out to get something for dinner, and before he left, he insisted that I choose what *we* have for dinner.

James has been nothing but a gentleman ever since I barrelled in the front door, soaking wet and miserable. But I couldn't help feeling like I was intruding on him. Invading his personal time away from the spotlight.

Of course, James hasn't given me any reason to think these things. If anything, he keeps finding reasons for us to spend more time together. Tonight, I'm taking him through a step-by-step beginner's guide to Spanish red wine – his idea, not mine!

My eyes close slowly and my body sinks into the most comfortable mattress I think I've ever slept on. The continuous rain splattering against the foggy window nurses me to sleep, and my subconsciousness takes over my thoughts.

There's James, tall and lean. Shit, James! Where's your shirt? His athletic body is rippled with cut muscles, his pecs firm. James smiles at me, the slight dimples on his cheeks buttoning his perfect browned skin. His eyes are the brightest of blue, making his messy blonde hair appear even lighter.

I feel myself drooling and when I wipe at my mouth, James reaches across and bats my hand away, insisting that he swipe the saliva from my lips.

"You're drooling," James says, and I feel him swipe at my mouth.

I feel him swipe at my mouth.

"Dinner's ready…"

My body shakes from side to side and my eyes open in a flash. I shoot up in bed, my neck snapping around. James is standing there before me, a bright red apron draped over his head, but he's shirtless underneath and the waist strap isn't tied around his hips. His nipples are visible on either side of the apron, and I reach up to my mouth where I swear he just mopped up my disgusting drool.

"Did you-" I grab at my mouth, my eyes wide and embarrassment gripping my mouth towards the floor.

James smiles, his cheeks dimpling just like they had seconds ago. Only now, there they are. There he is. Right in front of me.

In an apron.

Shirtless.

"No big deal," James says, tucking a handkerchief in the pocket on the front of the apron. "We had a mastiff when I was little, a little drool hasn't ever scared me off."

I'm doing my best to filter my red cheeks from James. He patted my drool away? Who does that?

I look down and my legs are twisted in the sheets and one side of my yoga pants is pushed up my leg, revealing my painfully white calves. *Shit, I wish I shaved my legs!* I see James following my gaze so I quickly divert his attention away from my gross hairy legs.

"Dinner's ready then?" I ask, kicking the sheets away and shuffling off the bed.

"Yep." James beams and my heart gives a little flutter.

Cut it out! You're killing me.

"I'll be down in a second, just give me a minute to freshen up," I say, pushing James out of the doorway.

"I was thinking, let's wear something nice…" James calls out from behind the closed door. "It's Valentine's Day after all… What do you think?"

"Ummmm…"

I look over my shoulder to my case which James had tossed on an overly large armchair. My stomach's sinking, making me feel suddenly nauseous. I hadn't planned on wearing anything but comfy pants and tank tops, baggy ones at that.

Sweat begins to bead on my forehead and I do that thing where I pace around in a tight circle. Valentines Day? Is this a date? He didn't mean it like that. I'm sure he didn't.

"I don't really have anything fancy," I call out, realising I had left James hanging for at least a minute now. "I'll see what I can do."

The best I could do was a silky night gown which might some-how resemble a dress if I tied it properly. No, that's silly. It's not a date.

Jeans – I have jeans. Jeans will do.

"OK. I'll change, too," James says.

I find myself wishing he didn't change, what's wrong with the apron and topless undershirt? I shake my head and remember the promise I made to Sophie. He's her brother and he's not available. At least, not for me. Not that he would want someone like me anyway. He's a star football player who could have any-one in England at the drop of a hat.

I hear his footsteps on the floorboards drifting off towards his bedroom and suddenly what I wear doesn't seem as important. Jeans and tank top it is. Remember, this isn't a date after all.

Is it?

I take my time to change and even though I've rallied myself up, telling myself it's not a date, I decide to do the decent thing for all womenkind, and shave my legs.

With a final glance in the freestanding mirror in the corner of the room, I suck in deep breaths and smile back at myself. My orange tank top is cut low into a v; my personal preference and nothing at all to do with trying to seduce James. I figure, with a body like mine, curves galore, why not get the girls out a bit? And hey, it's Valentine's Day! My black jeans are tight, so tight that I'm considering making the wine tasting one of those ones where you spit the wine out in a bowl instead of swallowing it. There's no room for bloating in here!

"I know you girls like to take your time, but the bangers are getting cold!" James' voice is deep and rattles up the narrow stairway.

"Bangers?" I call back, spraying my wrists with my favourite perfume, *Bloom Acqua* by Gucci. "You really cooked sausages?"

I step down the stairs and the smell drifting from the kitchen is like I'm back in the French cooking school that my parents sent me to when I was twelve. My nostrils come to life with the intoxicating smell of simmering white wine and garlic, and if my professionally trained chef's nose was telling me correctly, there was a hint of thyme and rosemary too.

"Sure as hell doesn't smell like bangers," I say, looking across the kitchen at James who is leaning over the stovetop.

He places the tongs on the bench and turns to face me. The red apron is half hanging over his body, but underneath he is wearing a buttoned white shirt. Small palm trees and coconuts dot the pressed fabric. The sleeves are short and instead of pants, he's got a pair of navy-blue chino shorts on. I take it in and find myself gawking at his huge calf muscles, realising for the first time in my life that I like a man with bulging calf muscles.

"You look…"

"Dreadful. Like I'm ready to get on a boat," James jokes, his smile as bright as my orange top. "Fucking Sophie got me these for Christmas, I look like a twat, but I didn't have much else."

If that's what twats look like these days, then I like twats.

"I know the feeling…" I run a hand down my front. "This is the best I could do."

"Don't be silly," James looks over and looks me up and down. The hair on my neck rises and a sudden wave of warmth flashes through my body. "You look stunning! Well done considering the circumstances."

I catch James looking at my chest and my back arches involuntary, making my already protruding bust pop out even more.

"Please, sit down."

James glides across the kitchen and pulls a chair out from under the small wooden dining table. A white table runner is centred lengthways across the top and cutlery has been set in two places opposite each other. A tall red candle flickers softly and sits off centre to two empty wine glasses that are turned upside down, just like Grant insists we have ours in the restaurant back in London.

"Now, *Bella…*" James fakes a Spanish accent, his hands flapping lazily in front of him as he speaks. He's cute, it's that boyish charm that has never faded, and when he rips the apron off, his shirt lifts up, showing his perfectly shaped butt in full, rounding his tight chinos. "Do we start with a Monastrell or Grenache? The dish is breast of chicken with a white, herbaceous sauce…"

I giggle at James' blatant mocking of a posh *maître d'*, but to be fair, he pulls it off. His nose is high in the air and he has pinched his fingers together tightly, looking more like an animated Italian than a Spanish waiter now.

"It would have to be the Grenache, for sure," I say, nodding firmly.

"Oh," James looks across at two bottles of wine on the edge of the bench, his playful mask falling. "Well, I didn't get that one, did I? Sounded weird. Will this do?"

A chesty laugh bursts from my body and I lose control. James' casual and relaxed nature feeds into me and his humour is so unique. His sense of humour is exactly like Sophie's and it's for that reason that we get along so well.

And that reason only, I swear.

He grabs the bottle on the left and pulls the cork out, turning the glasses up and pouring out the red wine. He dances back across to the stovetop and serves two steaming plates of delicious food that would be worthy to be served at the fancy Michelin-star dineries that dot the River Thames.

"This looks amazing," I gape, staring at the stunning plate of gorgeous food. "Where did you learn to cook like this?"

James smiles. "They made us do cooking classes when I was in the academy. They make sure you know how to eat right when you get home, especially as you grow up and move away from your parents. Sticking to your diet plan and all that… It all comes with being a professional athlete."

"Diet plan?"

"Oh yeah," James nods, his blue eyes looking at me from across the table. The flame from the candle glimmers in his eye and my heart does a weird flip. "They map everything out for you. School. Food. Education. You're an investment so they make sure you're doing everything properly."

James smiles and I stare back across at him. This was the same guy that I grew up with. He was gifted, that was for sure. Sports, cooking and even fashion! Despite the fact that his sister bought it for him, James wore those chinos and shirt like no other guy could.

But as I sat there, I struggled to believe that if he poked his head out the front door of this luxurious apartment in Brighton, a flock of fans would be hassling him within a few meters of the doorstep. His autograph was one of the most sought after in all of England. Forget the Queen. Forget Elton John or David Bowie.

Grown men would weep for James Hawkes to scribble on their shirt.

It was for that reason that I knew, without a doubt, that this wasn't a date. James could have anyone and he certainly wouldn't want a girl who was lumpy in all of the wrong places. He wouldn't want a lass who enjoys lounging around on weekends, binging Netflix or reading books. He wouldn't want a chef at a stupid wannabe French restaurant when he could be dating a supermodel from Argentina, jet setting around the world in private aeroplanes.

I cut the breast and forked a juicy mouthful into my gob, my heart snapping into a thousand tiny pieces at the sudden realization that this was never going to happen.

It is what it is.

It's not like it matters, I promised Sophie anyway. I should never have let the thought enter my mind.

"So, did you bring dessert?" James waggles his brows at me, and my brows furrow across at him.

There was no point.

Chapter Four

James

STARING ACROSS AT VICTORIA makes me conscious of how much of a pig I am when I eat. Sauce slopping everywhere... Disgusting chewing noises with each over-filled mouthful... The inability to belch with subtlety.

I make a conscious effort to slow down for the final few mouthfuls, and I reach out to down the last drop of red wine in my goblet when my plate is clear.

"This was amazing," Victoria says, dabbing a napkin at her mouth with the delicate class of a lass who knows how to dine out with elegance. "Thank you, James."

Victoria had been rather subdued ever since we sat down. Her larger-than-life smile faded shortly after she took the first mouthful of my cooking. Maybe I did an injustice to the food and her chef-y instincts were telling her not to eat it. Or perhaps she was just being kind when she said it looked amazing.

Did it look shit? Did I fuck it up?

Bloody hell. This was your chance to impress. To show her you're different to those other wankers.

"You're welcome," I say. I reach out for the bottle of wine. "More wine?"

Victoria looks up at me, her face sunken. I didn't know what the hell to do. Victoria was usually so full of life; she had been a pleasure to be around all afternoon. Her smile had its usual infectious, uplifting quality that drained any pressure from my everyday life away in an instant.

The whole day had been like the good old days when Sophie and her would pester me, nag me and bag me out. Only now, it was just me and her. There was no Sophie pulling Victoria away, yanking her upstairs, screaming at me that she was her friend and slamming the door shut so I couldn't gape at Victoria anymore.

"I think I'm OK, thanks," Victoria mumbles, her eyes searching the room.

"Alright…" I drag out.

I'm lost. I've fucked up. Dammit. This was my one shot.

I rise from my chair and grab Victoria's plate. She'd left behind a potato and a small bundle of green beans. Her chicken is gone but plenty of the sauce had been left behind. I place the dirty plates in the sink and clutch the second bottle of wine from the bench.

If this doesn't cheer her up, then I don't know what will.

"Come on," I wave, insisting Victoria joins me in the sitting room. "I'm not drinking this alone. I need a lesson in Spanish wine, remember?"

I sound pathetic. It's like I'm begging her to join me.

Victoria looks up at the wall where the clock shows us that it's only just past eight. The light from the kitchen filters out into the sitting room where the fireplace has been crackling away while we ate dinner. The windows are pitch black, but the rain continues to fall outside, softly kissing the window with a delicate pitter-patter.

"Perhaps a quick one," Victoria stands up and despite her subdued mood, my stupid cock thinks that's an invitation to join the party. Her body is so grand, and those jeans are gripping her hips in a way that makes my hands twitch with anticipation every time I look at them. "Then I'd better get some rest. That's what I'm here for after all…"

Victoria squeezes past me in the doorway, making my dick jerk again and I have no shame in admitting that I watch her ass wobble the length of the room as she heads straight across for the fireplace.

She turns her back on it and it's then that I decide not to switch the light on. The orange glow in the room is enough to make out her gorgeous face. All I need to see is those glowing cheeks blushing with a soft pink flush. If only I could lift her spirits, I could spend the rest of the night staring at her plump, full lips as she talks so passionately about her life.

I walk across, sliding the door to the kitchen so the sitting room darkens further. Victoria remains standing in front of the fireplace, her back to the flames and an empty wine glass in her hand.

"Here."

If she drinks enough maybe she'll forget about whatever is troubling her. Maybe, just maybe she'll start laughing again.

I hold out the bottle and pour slowly. My eyes drift from the glass and I find myself staring at Victoria. Her sweet smell is stronger in here where the aroma of dinner isn't as prominent. I take in deep breaths and struggle to remove my eyes from her…

"James! JAMES!"

Victoria jumps back and her hand swipes down her front. A broad wine stain soaks into her orange top just below her breasts. I panic and my head races, blurring my vision. A dark red stain quickly forms on Victoria's outfit and I've turned to jelly.

"Oh shit!" I shout, sinking back and thumping the bottle of wine down on the coffee table. "Victoria! I'm so sorry. Sorry! Sorry! Sorry!"

I pace around, panicked and I have no fucking idea what to do. Victoria is calmly dabbing at her top with her hand and I'm running around like the fucking chicken that we just ate would have been before the farmer grabbed it.

"What do I do? Tell me what to do and I'll do it!" My voice is rushed, and my chest is so tight that I'm finally using the breathing exercises the coaches have been raving on about.

I want to help, but I have no fucking clue how to.

"It's fine," Victoria smiles, although her brow pulls together slightly when she sees me breathing deeply, counting to three and then exhaling over and over again.

Suddenly I stop.

She smiled.

"It's just wine, Jame," she says, and her words floated across the room and kissed my ears.

My heart lifts and the adrenaline racing through my veins is instantly extinguished.

"Jame?" I say, my voice soft.

Victoria looks up, realising what she had just said. Her green eyes dart sideways, lingering on me only for a moment before dancing around the room again.

"No one calls me that anymore either," I utter, unable to retract my gaze from Victoria.

"Oh," she hums, her hand still dabbing at her top.

The stain is still growing, and I look down at the bottle. There was at least a quarter gone and Victoria's glass was only half filled. How much did I slop on her?

God you're a dick.

Finally getting over myself, I race into the kitchen to grab a towel and return as quickly as possible to Victoria.

"Here, see if this helps…" I hold out the towel, but the damage has been done. "I'm so sorry. I don't know what happened. I'll… I'll… I'll get you a new top!"

I knew exactly what happened, but it wasn't like I could tell her that I was lost in her dreamy eyes.

"Really, James, it's OK. This is an old top. I was only going to turf it when I got back to London anyway," Victoria admits, shrugging her shoulders. She offers a smile that melts my legs to jelly again.

"Fine then. At least let me soak it for you. We might save it!"

Without giving her a chance to reply, I step in closer and suddenly my chest pulls together, constricting tighter and tighter with every closing inch that I draw nearer to Victoria's body. Her eyes are wide, and as I move in closer, I swear she stops breathing.

"I'll hold this, you take your top off," I say, grabbing her wine glass and moving to place it down beside the bottle.

"What?" Victoria splutters out and she stumbles backwards. "Oh no, no, no, no, no… I'll go upstairs and change."

"Oh, come on, I've seen plenty of women in their bra's befor e… What's the big deal?"

"Yeah, but you've never seen *me* in *my* bra before*!*" Victoria stammers out, her eyes growing wider and wider. "That's a sight no one needs to see, believe me!"

"Don't be ridiculous! You're beautiful, Victoria!"

Victoria huffs. "Oh, yeah, ok! That's why I can't get a second date! Because I'm beautiful… Is that the reason all of those guys insist on ordering my meals for me, too?"

"Listen to me, Victoria. There is nothing wrong with you. Trust me."

I pin her with a firm look but I know my words are being wasted. She pops out a hip and crosses her arms over her chest.

"You have to say that; Sophie would kill you if you said otherwise."

I shake my head firmly. "Believe me, Sophie has nothing to do with this. Now come on, we can still save this top."

I'd heard enough and I hustle her. Not taking no for an answer, I begin pulling at the bottom of the orange cotton that's tucked so elegantly into those tight jeans. After a deep sigh, Victoria goes along with it, if she batted away my hands, then so be it. I would stop. There is no way I would force Victoria to do anything.

But she doesn't.

Instead, she tugs at the top around her waist, lifting it up and over her head with a swift flick.

Oh fuck… Oh fuck… Oh fuck!

Victoria was right. I hadn't ever seen her in her bra before. And what a fantastic sight it was. I mean, her lush curves had always driven me crazy. She's got shape. She's more than a handful in all the right places. And I fucking love it.

My hands are shaking. I grab the tank top and Victoria shuffles across to the coffee table to retrieve her glass without looking at me. Her eyes are hiding away, and she lifts her glass to her lips and drags a swig, stopping for a second to draw breath, before downing the remainder of the wine in her glass.

I smile and grab the bottle from the table, pouring, ever so carefully, to top her up and doing the same for myself.

"Stand back," I joke, and when Victoria giggles softly, my ears prick. I have to keep her smiling, so I do my best to think on the spot. "So… que pasa? Si un e tado…"

I hold my glass up and swirl the red contents around, looking up through the bottom of the glass with squinted eyes. I pretend to be intense and study the wine before my eyes with the interest of an expert, hoping my foolishness is lightening the tense mood gripping the room.

A giggle from beside me lifts my spirits. It's working. After the grump she's been in since we started dinner, I felt like John-fucking-Lennon for making her laugh when she's feeling down. I lower the glass down before I spill it everywhere again, drawing in a giant gulp that empties half of the tumbler.

"You're an idiot, you know that?" Victoria says, looking briefly across at me before stumbling a few steps sideways. She sips her wine with much more class than her last effort and her luscious lips lock on the rim of the glass, leaving behind a red stain of lipstick.

I observe her from a few feet away, unable to remove my eyes more than ever before. As if she can feel me staring, Victoria moves her arm across her exposed skin as if to hide it from my searching eye.

She gulps down another large mouthful and looks past me to the doorway.

"Right. I'm going to get another top," Victoria says, taking a step sideways.

"Why?" I say, my voice suddenly dropping to a whisper.

"I'm not staying like this! You don't need to see me half naked while you're trying to relax…" Victoria crosses her other arm across her body and my head begins to shake.

"Don't start this again…" I step forward, unable to control my legs. Maybe it's the wine, maybe I'm just tired of lying to myself but my thoughts begin to take control of my tongue. "What if I *want* to see it?"

"You don't want to see this, James…"

Victoria steps back but I catch her by the waist and pull her in. My fingers grip into the curves of her hips, half touching her bare skin, the other half pulling at the loopholes of her jeans. Our bodies are close together and my head is inches from Victoria's. I can feel her nervous breath on my face, and my eyes are directly staring in hers.

The fireplaces cracks loudly beside us, but we don't move.

The world around us doesn't exist.

"James, what are you doing?" Victoria whispers, her voice so quiet it's almost silent.

"What I should have done a long time ago."

Chapter Five
Victoria

JAMES IS KISSING ME. James is kissing me! James FUCKING Hawkes is kissing me!

You know that thing that you build up in your head for years and years and you make out like it's the thing that's been missing from your life? If you could just get that *thing* in your life, nothing else would matter. Happiness would no longer escape your clutches. Joy would be attained instantly once you get *that thing*.

It turns out, James' tongue rattling against mine was exactly how I had imagined it.

Warm. Intense. *Strong.*

"Oh, fuck," James groans, lifting his wet lips from mine, only long enough for the words to fumble from his mouth and his eyes to sink in mine. "You taste so fucking good."

"Mmmm hmmm…"

I simply groan a response and yank his head back on mine with a firm hand on the back of his head. I feel like I'm ripping the hair on the back of his head out, but he's never allowed to leave. He's mine now.

Shit. But what about Sophie?

"Oh God," I choke, James' teeth tugging at my bottom lip as I speak.

"I know," James groans again. "You're so fucking hot."

"No… No we can't… We can't…"

My hands press against James' chest, the prickling sensation that's shooting up my arm doesn't aid me in my attempt to push him away. My body wants this. *I want this.*

But Sophie. The promise.

"Your sister," I mumble, my lip drawn in between my teeth as I savour his taste.

James lifts my chin with a firm finger underneath my chin. Our eyes lock and I hate that he's torturing me like this. This is all I've ever dreamt of. This is every curvy girls dream, right? He's a fucking footballer for goodness sake! England's number one! And I'm rejecting him?! Maybe my brother is right, maybe I do need to seek help. I'm clearly fucking mental.

"Sophie? That's who you're thinking about right now?" James' face is scrunched, but he still looks as handsome as ever. He's still clinging to my body, only now, his hands are pressing down on my shoulders, as if he's afraid I'm about to do a runner.

"Well yeah!" I step back, breaking our connection. "I told her I wouldn't ever go there with you."

"You did?" James' brow arches and his deep blue eyes widen. "How and why would that ever come up?"

"I don't know," I shrug, realising that I'm still sporting just a bra so I pull my arms down and cover my exposed belly. "I guess that's what girls do when they have brothers. I made her do the same for Harry."

James stares at me for a moment. There's a silence and another crack of the fireplace echoes around the room, only this time I jump about a foot back. James smiles, and I'm suddenly grateful for the break in tension.

"We're adults now… We're not kids anymore. We're not jealous siblings who bicker over who gets to hang around who, or who's friend is who…"

James steps in closer and suddenly I get the feeling that he's not going to give up that easily. His eyes have a different look about them; they've narrowed and turned to slits and they're pinning me to the spot. It's like he's wanted this for as long as I have.

But that can't be right, can it?

I can't move. I don't want to move.

"Tell me you don't want this," James whispers and he reaches out, his hand grazing against my cheek as he tucks a strand of dark hair behind my ear. "If you can tell me you don't want this then I'll stop right now."

His voice is raspy and hot on my face and the orange glow of the fire flickers light and dark on his cheek. He closes in and our bodies touch. My bust pushes against his hard pecs. He wraps his hands around my hips again and heaves me forward with a force that makes all air escape my lungs. I can feel his hardness against the outside of my jeans.

I'm breathless.

I'm a goner.

My lips crash against his again and we start back where we left. James takes control of the kiss only this time he's pushing me back to the sofa as we lash our wet tongues against each other. Holy shit can he kiss. My stomach is swirling and twirling with each swiping motion his tongue works against mine and when we crash down on the couch, I'm able to come up for air.

"Shit," I pant. "Shit. James. Are we doing this?"

James stalks over me and rips his shirt off. The pecs that felt so firm against me break free from his shirt. They're matched for chiselled lines only by his cut six-pack. Oh, and the 'V' on his waistline is guiding my hands exactly to where they want to be.

"We're doing this Victoria,' James says, standing over me with a bulge tenting his sports trousers so far from his waist, that scouts could camp under there. "I've waited too long for this."

My chest is pulsing. I've never felt like this. Now I'm wishing I did have something nicer to wear to dinner. It's fucking Valentine's weekend and I'm on a getaway weekend… Why didn't I pack for the unexpected?

Maybe because this has never happened to me before. And it might not ever happen again.

I'm short of breath and I wish that my eyes would stop blurring. This might be the one and only time I'm with James-fucking-Hawkes.

James Hawkes is hovering over me, drinking in my body with a thirst in his eyes. *My body.*

"You're fucking perfect," James groans, and his hands finally move down my body.

He starts at my chest, pulling at my bra to expose a nipple. He lowers himself down to his knees, I'm half on the couch, half hanging off it. My legs are spread, and he's positioned himself between them, and now…

"Oh, shit…"

He takes my hardened nipple in his mouth. His tongue swirls around my breast, while the other works over the button on my jeans. I feel it pop and before I can lift my ass off the couch, my pants are nearly off.

"You move quickly," I tease.

"Don't be so impressed," James says, his hands rubbing up my legs so they tingle. "You're so fucking perfect that I'm just trying to hold it together long enough to get you yours."

"Don't worry about me…"

Something takes over my body and I reach out for James and pull him on me. He's kissing me and I tug at his trousers, lifting the band over his large erection so they fall to the floor. His pants follow quickly, and my hands are quickly gripping his cock.

"OH!" James' body jerks and I feel his dick pulse in my hands. "SHIT!"

His body is hovering over mine and my ass is perched on the edge of the couch. My hand jacks him. Full stroke after full stroke. He's long, and though I don't have much to compare it to, the girth is very, *very* impressive. It's perfect, and I take a good look before looking up to his hooded eyes.

"Taste me," James looks down at me, and I know he's not asking. "Taste me, baby. Tell me if you like it."

I nod and give one final stroke, pulling his cock back as I reposition myself on the sofa. James' head is looking up to the ceiling and when I take him in my mouth, I'm not sure who let out the louder groan.

It feels hot and firm against my tongue. I swipe and stroke and when he grips my hair and balls it in a tight fist, slight shoots of pleasurable pain sting my scalp and I know I'm doing it just right. His hips pump and I feel his cock grinding against the walls of my mouth.

"Oh, you take it good, baby," James groans. My hands have worked their way around to his butt, and I clasp firmly as he thrusts his cock deeper down my throat. "You take it *so* good."

He pumps faster and when I feel his cock tensing in my mouth, I can almost hear the warning bells ringing in his head.

"Shit!" James cries out and he pulls his dick from my mouth. "Oh, god! I'm… I'm…"

He's stroking himself in front of me and I've never been more turned on in my life. His eyes are wide now and the veins running the length of his forearm have formed ridges. He locks his gaze on my chest and I shuffle forward, wrapping my hand around his as he strokes.

I have no idea what I'm doing, but I make sure my previously unexposed breast is out by tugging my bra strap over my shoulder, loosening its grip on my chest. I grab my breasts and circle them around his cock, rubbing gently.

My tits are out now and James stares at them as he strokes faster and faster, eventually rocking his head back as white, creamy pleasure escapes from his throbbing hardness, covering my tits with three, maybe four hard pulses.

"Fuuuccckk!" James screams and I swear the wine glasses on the table rattle together.

The warmth against my chest is odd. It's a warm sensation that I never knew I would ever get to experience. I can feel it running over my right breast, its heat pulling over my hard nipple like flowing lava. But the more I watch it drip, and the longer James stands there, finishing himself with a final few squeezes of his cock, slapping the last drops against my breasts, the more turned on I get.

I've never felt it like this before. I've never done anything like this before.

But oh my. Oh god. Am I turned on.

"I'm so sorry," James pants, looking down at me with his tongue half hanging out of his mouth. "I couldn't hold it. Do you know how long I've been dreaming of doing that for?"

I don't offer a reply, I'm too busy looking at my drenched tits, gaping at his pleasure running down my body.

"We're not done. I'm not finished with you." James says and I look up at him, my stomach suddenly lifting.

I gulp down. I'm relieved… I mean, my pussy is so wet right now that I'm sure I might need to break the suction when I stand up from the couch. But if that was all I ever got with James Hawkes, then his cum on my chest was a hell of a lot more than I thought I would ever get anyway.

"Oh really?" I taunt, trailing a finger up James' hip, making his body wiggle a cold shiver.

I flutter my lashes at him in a way that I never have to any guy ever before. I'm not sure what it is about him, but goddamn, James makes me feel sexier than I've ever felt before in my life.

"You're not getting out of it that easy, Victoria…" James steps back and his cock is still rock hard. "Meet me upstairs in… 15 minutes."

Chapter Six

James

I HUSTLE AROUND MY room, every few seconds glancing at the clock on my bedside table.

Two minutes and she'll be here.

When we set off in different directions at the top of the stairs, Victoria agreed to meet me in my room. I hadn't wasted any time lighting the candles on my dresser that, despite my protests, Mom had put there as 'decorations' years ago. Finally, they served a purpose as they lit my bedroom with seductive orange hue.

Thanks, Mom.

I rummage through my dresser after splashing a dash of cologne around my neck, searching for silky black boxers. It's best I can do; I hadn't planned on any of this but watching my spunk drip down Victoria's amazing curves had me itching for more.

My cock remains firm, and when the floorboards in the hallway creak, it gives an excited twitch. My heart skips a beat with each of the three gentle knocks at my bedroom door. It's a quiet, nervous knock, but Victoria has nothing to worry about. I'm about to take care of her, just like I had dreamed about for too long now.

"Come in," I call out, perching myself on the corner of the bed after quickly pulling the boxers on.

"I didn't have anything nice, so don't-" Victoria's soft voice is only just audible through the door.

"I'm sure you looking stunning, just come in!" I say, my eyes glued to the door handle which isn't turning.

"Just don't get your hopes up, Mister," Victoria says.

"Mister? Ooo, I like that, baby," I tease.

The door swings open, and my jaw drops. For someone who didn't bring anything sexy, Victoria is sure as shit pulling it off.

"Oh fuck," I choke, my eyes wide. "And you didn't bring any-thing nice?"

Victoria is in a dressing gown that's tightly wrapped around her body, hugging all her delicious curves. Her lips dark red with her signature lipstick colour, the same colour that I had just washed off my cock. Her nipples are protruding through the pink silk, and judging by the swelling in the gown, her bra is no longer in the way on her enormous bust.

She steps over, one leg swinging out in front of the other like she's Victoria-fucking-Beckham on the catwalk. Her eyes lock on mine, her bright green eyes slanted with a yearning of years and years of ignoring the sparks that had finally unleashed between us.

I stood up, my arms reaching out for the black ribbon that sealed the gown together, hiding everything I desired behind the sexy, silky curtain of her robe. My fingers pull the knot in the centre and the two sides open up, revealing a body like I haven't ever seen before.

"Commando?" I say, eyeballing Victoria's naked body. The gown drops to the floor.

"Well, unless you think comfy couch underwear is sexier than this…"

"Oh, no," I shake my head ferociously. "No, no, no… No, this is perfect."

My excited hands run the length of her body. I cup Victoria's breasts, large and round. Then her hips, perfectly leading my hands down to a well-tamed pussy, my fingers caressing a light layer of fluff above the folded fleshy lines that hide away that bulging hood at the center of her pleasure.

It's that center that is making my mouth water.

I want to taste it so bad.

"Lay down," I pull at Victoria, my hands gripping her hips above her naked ass. She collapses to the bed and, as if I was on the field, leading England to glory, I take control. "Spread them."

I lean down, rocking back on my heels, my eyes drinking in the folds of beauty as my hands press her legs apart.

Holy glory. Glory, glory, glory.

I draw in a breath and Victoria giggles. Her hand reaches out to the top of my head and grips my hair hard while guiding my face to her pussy.

My tongue plunges inside her and the candle flickers in the room like a rod of lightning just cracked between us. My tongue dives deeper, lapping at her warm treasure and I can taste her pleasure swimming inside of her.

"Oh god," Victoria groans and her hand pulls at my hair. "Oh… James!"

I don't know if she's asking for my attention, but I don't stop. This is too good. Her pussy is in control now.

Forget the England team. Forget football. Forget anything.

I just want this pussy against my mouth.

I push my tongue firmly against her clit and her groan of pleasure gives me the motivation to insert one finger inside her warmth. Another finger follows and I begin to work them inside her, grinding against her tight walls with a curling motion deep inside her.

"James! Oh fuck!" Victoria hunches up on the bed, using her elbows to perch herself up so she's got a better view of me devouring her sopping wet entrance.

My two fingers dive deeper and deeper while my tongue flaps viciously against her. I feel a bump inside her and rub it with two fingers, knowing full well her g-spot has been found and, like a fucking astronaut on a newly discovered planet, I'm planting my flag and making it my own with each hard rub against it.

"Oh shit, yes! Oh, James! Yes!" Victoria's voice has risen to new levels, each word breathless and I feel her insides clenching. "It's coming! Don't st-"

Victoria's breath ceases and she collapses back on the bed. Her hips begin thrusting against my hand. I don't move, my tongue and fingers remaining in place while her climax constricts my fingers inside her.

"OHHHHH, JAMES!"

My scalp stings with pain as Victoria grips my hair harder with every pulsing movement her hips shudder. Lucky Sophie isn't here, she would be able to hear Victoria's personal announcement of pleasure way down at the pier. I lick softly and aid Victoria back down from her peak, pecking the inside of her hips gently.

"Did I pull your fucking hair out?" Victoria's eyes finally open and pop up between her legs, looking down her sexy body to see me remaining between her legs.

"No," I wink, shooting up from my heels to lift Victoria and throw her back further on the bed. I crawl across the sheets to her, my hardness doing it's best to escape from the constraints of my silky boxers. "Not yet, anyway. I'm not even close to being finished with you."

I stand on the bed, my frame towering over Victoria who is laying below me, studying every inch of my body. I yank at the waistline of my boxers and my hard erection bursts from the fabric.

Despite already having it halfway down her throat less than an hour ago, Victoria can't take her eyes off my length.

"You like this baby?"

I remain standing above her and grab my cock, watching her squirm with every stroke that I tease her with. She nods and I see her tongue swipe across her lip while her hands move down to her large breasts. I stroke again but a sudden wave of pleasure pulsing through me makes me rethink my strategy.

I'm not blowing early again. Get inside her, now!

I drop to the bed and Victoria's eyes light up. My legs are spread so I'm positioned correctly and the soft light in the room is enough for me to see the moisture dripping from her pleasure centre. Victoria's hands are still cupping her breasts and her eyes are half-lidded, waiting.

I shuffle forward and aim my cock at the centre, feeling that pulse through my body that I'm doing my best to control. I press ahead, my knob touching her wetness and suddenly a thought rushes through my head.

"Shit! A condom!" I sit back on my heels, my stomach sinking.

Victoria smiles. "I'm on the pill, forget it. I want you. I want you now. Bareback. I want to *feel* you. Please…"

Oh god, stop.

The pressure building in my groin is already becoming too much, and now Victoria is practically begging me to fuck her. Her lashes flutter at me and I gulp down.

There's no stopping now and I grip myself, notching my hardness against her wet pussy. This was going to be quick; I knew it. My cock won't stop fucking pulsing.

And God damn, look at her!

I take the plunge, my cock feeling the warmth of her oozing wetness as she takes the entire length in one, long, deep thrust. My hips sink into Victoria, and instantly my world is changed forever.

Her eyes close over, her teeth biting down as I pull back and thrust again. Her breasts sway with every bed rattling movement my hips drive into her. My heart is beating heavily inside my chest like it hasn't ever before. My breath is short, and I can't stop staring at Victoria's eyes as I plunge deeper and deeper inside her.

This is what has been missing from my life.

There's a connection.

There's intimacy.

There's… *love?*

"Yes! Oh, yes!" Victoria screams, and she's grinding her hips against me so I'm filling her completely.

"You take it so good, baby," I moan, my hand gripping her curvy hips with a full handful. "Your body. Oh god. Oh… Your pussy! Your pussy is so tight and…"

"James! Oh!" Victoria's mouth gapes and my cock feels the tensing inside her. "I'm coming again!"

"Shit!"

I collapse down so my body is layering Victoria's with a blanket of pleasure. Our naked chests grind against each other, and my hips are almost attacking her center like it's an open goal and I need to finish the game.

"Fuuuuuuuckkk!"

There it is. The tensing has built up and now the release is worth every torturing second of trying to hold it back. My cock bursts inside Victoria and her fingernails dive into my hips as she locks her teeth into the side of my neck, muffling the escaping screams of our simultaneous climax.

"Fuck, James! FUCK!"

Chapter Seven

Victoria

"I DIDN'T THINK YOU'D be a snuggly sleeper…" James teases.

The room has a soft, natural light filling it and my eyes are taking time to adjust. I've just woken up and there's a wet patch on my cheek. It's got nothing to do with James, even though his arms are tightly wrapped around me, and his cock is pressing into my back.

Nope. Unfortunately, it's my own drool.

Dammit. You have to stop dribbling in your sleep! It's embarrassing!

"This is… nice." I say, wiping the drool on my cheek on the pillow. "Whoever thought I'd be waking up next to James Hawkes?"

James laughs; his voice is a sexier level of deep first thing in the morning. "Why do you call me that now?"

"Well, that's who you are. The media's favourite son. *England's* favourite…"

"And now your favourite?"

James' lips press against my naked shoulder and for the first time since I've opened my eyes, I come to the realization that I'm *still naked*.

My blood chills and I grip the sheets up so my body is covered. The wine has worn off now, and suddenly I'm self-conscious of my body again. What if James sees me in the daylight and he regrets everything? He wouldn't be the first man after a one-night stand to race out of the room right before my eyes, hoping to hell that I was still asleep so I didn't see the look of regret filling their sorry-ridden eyes.

"It's still fucking raining," James peaks out of the window and as he does so, his hand drops down to just above my groin, making it tingle again. "What are we going to do today?"

"We?" I ask.

"We?" A voice that isn't mine, nor James', makes my stomach drop as it mimics my words with a hint of venom.

It came from the doorway, and I roll over to see Sophie standing against the frame of the door, her arms folded over her chest and her eyes cutting across at me, narrowed and wild.

She's pissed and her eyes are firmly locked on me.

"Soph! What are you doing here?" I shoot up and grip the sheets, covering my body.

"Ruining your *romantic* weekend by the seems of it!" Sophie snaps, and it's a tone that I've heard before, but it's never been directed at me.

James is fumbling around beside me but he's not helping.

"It isn't what it looks like, please," I beg, wishing now more than ever that I wasn't fucking naked.

"Really?" Sophie bows her head, her eyes pinning me to the bed with a hard look. "Because it looks like my best friend is in bed with my brother… Even though she's sworn that she would *never, ever* do that to me."

James has jumped up from bed, his bare ass not aiding the situation as Sophie's eye catch his white ass cheeks and she retches and turns her back. He's fumbling on the floor and finally he pulls up a pair of denim jeans. I take the opportunity of Sophie's turned back to jump out from behind the sheets and wrap myself in the silky gown that was passionately dropped to the floor last night.

"Sophie," James says, storming across the room to his sister. "Really… it's not what it looks like. We didn't plan this. It just happened. I came here to escape, and Victoria said you gave her a set of keys. We didn't plan on being here together. We had some dinner and waaaaay too much wine, and it just sort of… happened. I didn't mean to. You have to believe me."

James's words cut me in half and I'm fumbling around the room to escape.

He regrets it! He fucking regrets it! I knew it.

Tears swell in the corners of my eyes, and I want to get the hell out of here. It meant nothing to him. He was just drunk.

I race across to the door and force my way past Sophie, warm tears now falling down my cheeks.

"Move," I demand, one hand gripping my gown tight the other shoving Sophie aside.

"Where are you going?" I hear James call out, but everything is just a blur.

"Victoria! Don't you dare leave!" Sophie snorts, but I slam my bedroom door closed and begin throwing everything in my case through blurred vision.

I dress as quickly as possible and ignore the echoing voices in the hallway, I race downstairs and burst through the front door.

I should never have opened myself up like that. I thought he actually wanted me. But like all the men before him, he didn't want *me*. He just wanted his fucking dick wet.

The worst part is, I thought I could actually convince my best friend that me being in love with James would be a good thing for us and our friendship.

I was in love with him. I *am* in love with him. My best friend's brother.

There was no doubt about that now. I knew it. I always have been.

But now, he's broken my fucking heart.

Chapter Eight

James

"Fucking hell, Sophie!" I scream, and the slam of the front door makes my eyes clench shut.

"What?" Sophie gasps, her brows halfway up her face. "You're the asshole here. Not me."

Her mask of innocence isn't fooling me.

I'm standing staring at the door. Victoria's gone and I'm left here to deal with my stupid sister alone. I needed Victoria. Not only to help me talk some sense in to Sophie, but I needed her to complete me.

My temper is rising, so I turn to Sophie and point to the sitting room. "Go. We're going to sort this out once and for all. If we're lucky, we might be able to catch her after I'm finished with you."

I push Sophie's shoulder, so she turns in the right direction, and I follow her steps towards the sofa opposite the now extinguished fireplace. Sophie slumps down on the sofa, her foot tapping as she holds her arms firmly across her chest. Her face is glum, and I know my sister well enough to approach this in the right way: all guns blazing.

"What you saw up there…"

The words rush from my lips. I know Victoria is on the move. And trains to London are so frequent that I only had half an hour, at the most, to convince Sophie that this was a good thing.

"You weren't meant to see it."

"Oh, gee, you think…" Sophie rolls her eyes. "You've been headbutting too many footballs, either that or you're just thick… She's my best fr-"

"I know that, Sophie!" I interrupt, it's the only way I'll get my point across over my sister. "I know she is! But I'm in love with her!"

A double-decker bus zooms past the window, and the ringing bells of a group of cyclists outside on the street break the silence gripping the room. Sophie's just staring at me like she's waiting for me to burst out laughing. Like this is just some joke to me and I've happily taken advantage of her best friend for my own sick benefit.

"You're… You're in love with her?" Sophie asks, quietly.

"Yes. I'm in love with Victoria." My head confirms with a stern nod. I glance at the clock on the wall. *Fuck.* "Always have been. Ever since you bought her home from school and introduced her to Mom and Dad."

"We were only thirteen or something…"

"I know," A smile tugs at my lips, the memory is one of the happiest I can recall. That was the day I started believing in love at first sight. "I was fifteen and I still remember the chocolate stain you and Victoria were begging Mom to help you remove from her school blazer… Otherwise her parents would kill her."

"Fucking hell. I forget how batshit crazy her mom is…" Sophie laughs and shakes her head, her lip softening slightly. "And so, what… I'm supposed to believe that this isn't just you being a stupid boy, using my best friend to get…"

Sophie's eyes glance down at my crotch, and I think for a moment, she forgets that I'm her brother and she's staring at my groin.

"Ew! Ew!" Sophie's body shivers and it's my turn to roll my eyes at her, giving her a shove for being so childish. "You really love her?"

I nod. "Like nothing else in the world."

"Wow," Sophie says, falling back on the couch. "I didn't know."

I move down and sit beside her, one eye on the clock and one on Sophie.

A deep breath fills my lungs and I'm doing everything I can to shove down the rising vile that's making its way up my throat. It's too much. My hands are shaking and sweat has begun to form across my forehead. I'm overheating.

When I woke this morning, I had everything I ever dreamed of. There she was… In my arms. Where she belonged. Where *we* belonged. Together. For one night, my world was complete.

The thought of never kissing those lips again… Never hearing her sweet voice singing my name… That smile from across the table or those lips leaving lipstick staining the glassware…

My entire world was escaping my clutches.

And if I didn't act swiftly, it would be gone.

"I've been trying to hide it for years. I thought it would pass, you know? I figured I was just some silly teenage boy… It was just a crush. A weird attraction to my sister's friend." I shook my head and stared in to the distance. "But it didn't."

"We had an agreement which probably didn't help you either…" Sophie says, turning to face me. "We promised-"

"To never touch each other's brothers… I know. Victoria said so last night."

"But she just went and did it anyway!"

"Yes, Sophie," I snap quickly, trying my best to reel the calmness back into the conversation. I was winning Sophie over I couldn't afford to go backwards; Victoria would be at the station by now. "Because I said you'd be understanding. You wouldn't stand in the way of two people who loved each other."

Sophie's brows shot up again and she moved to the edge of the sofa. "You think she loves you, too?"

A sudden clenching grips my insides and twists. If she had asked me last night, I would have said yes… without a doubt, Victoria loves me. But now? The look Victoria gave me as she slammed the door shut, tears staining those precious cheeks… I wasn't so sure.

"There's only one way to find out, right?" I say, a hint of hope lifting my voice, inviting Sophie to join me on the sprint I was about to make to the station.

Sophie stumbled over a deep breath. Her eyes flicked from the window to me and then back again. I could almost read her thoughts. If she agreed to come with me, there was no going back. Not for her. Not for anyone.

But what if she doesn't agree?

My head is a mess and I begin to pace around the room. Sophie is deep in thought and not offering a word. I can literally hear the clock ticking and every stroke of the second hand is a second wasted. Images of Victoria boarding the train at the station flash through my head. The imaginary sight of Victoria with a suitcase in one hand and a wet tissue dabbing her at her eyes in the other makes my entire body tense up.

Maybe I'm not OK with accepting no as an answer. I've taken the plunge and I know the connection with Victoria is real.

So what if Sophie can't deal with it?

It's my life… It's Victoria's life.

And if Sophie can't handle it then maybe that's her problem and not ours…

"Sophie!" I yell, my impatience causing my hands to ball into fists. "Are you OK with this? I'm not letting her get away from me. Not anymore."

Sophie presses her hands to her knees, and she rises, standing up straight before me.

"Let's go get her."

Chapter Nine

"… Please mind the gap… Train approaching… Mind the gap… North bound to Highbury and Islington via London Central…"

I swipe at my eyes. They must be glowing fucking red by now and I'm growing tired of the man across the platform who is refusing to pull his stare from me, despite the constant daggers I've aimed at him.

I'm saturated. Again.

The stupid rain pelted down with every fastened step that I ran, yes ran (!!!), to the station. I had to get out of there and if that meant running for the first time since primary school then so be it. That's just what I had to do to escape the confined walls of the apartment. The apartment where I shared the moment of my life with…

"James?" My eyes widen so far that the cold air stings my irises.

"Fuck," James puffs, collapsing his hands on his knees. He's panting so hard the steam from his breath surrounds us like a hovering cloud of fog.

"Bloody hell, and you call yourself a professional athlete…"

Sophie's voice catches me off-guard, and I swing around to see my best friend, or ex-best friend perhaps, lagging behind her brother. Her dark hair is slicked to her face, long, wet and dripping like a drowned puppy dog.

"Oh, you can talk… I didn't think you were ever going to cross at that crossing…" James scoffs, his hair also drenched.

"Well I'm not a fucking lunatic like you! It was a fucking lorry you twat!" Sophie yells, her cheeks wet and red. "Who runs out in front of a lorry! Seriously."

James goes to yell back but he catches my eye, and the thought seems to escape his mind. I gulp down. What the hell is he doing here? I was just a root. He'd said as much, so why was he running after me?

"Victoria…" James steps in closer to me and over his shoulder I see the train finally pulling in and blocking out the creep across the platform. "Victoria, please…"

"What, James?"

I am trying my best to look everywhere except at James. I know if I look at him, I'll just forget it all. I'll forget what he said and how he raced to make excuses as to why he had been caught in bed with me.

If I look at him again, I'll just stare into those eyes, and they will swarm over my every fibre and consume me again.

Just like they always had.

"Just wait, would you?" James' hand brushes against my arm, holding me from lifting the handle on my suitcase. "Please."

And there it is. His eyes pin me to the spot and my legs may as well have a rope tied around them. I'm not moving.

The loud squeak of the train coming to a halt pierces the air, and a crowd of Londoners boarding the train back north file along the yellow line on the edge of the platform. Sophie is busy draining her hair of rain, a small puddle forming on the floor underneath her knee-length boots.

"James… What's the point?"

James steps up and grabs my hands. His warm palms cup them as he pulls them up to his chest, holding them oh so close to him.

Fucking stop it! This is torture.

"I need to tell you something… Something I should have told you years ago. There's things that need saying after last night, and I'm not sure what I said earlier came across so well."

My brows shoot up and an involuntary scoff leaves my throat. Sophie is staring at James as intently as I am, and I wonder why the fuck she's here. Maybe she is just making sure he swears off me for good? Maybe she won't take his word for it if he says he's told me to leave him the fuck alone. She's making sure the job is finished and his torture of me is complete.

"OK," I breath, deciding it's better to just rip the band aid off. "Fine. Let's hear it."

James looks to his feet and draws in the deepest breath. His chest protrudes between our bodies and his hands are still clasping mine, but why? My heart is pounding so fast that I can barely hear the shuffling of hundreds of travellers surrounding the station, let alone James' voice which starts to vibrate through me.

"About the same time that you swore to Sophie that you wouldn't ever get involved with each other's brothers, I developed a crush on you. I was instantly attracted to you, but I knew it would never happen. I mean, look at you…" James' eyes rolled over my body, drinking me in just like he did last night. My hands were now sweating so much that I felt them slip in his. "You're beautiful, Victoria, even with a chocolate stain splattered on your blazer…"

"Chocolate stain?" I swallow hard, looking down the front of me expecting to see a chocolate stain on my wet clothing. "What the hell are you talking about?"

"You burst through the front door. It was the first time I had ever laid eyes on my sister's infamous friend, *Victoria.* She never shut up about you and finally I knew why. Bright red hair. The darkest green in your eyes that I had ever seen… Sophie was all up in Mom's face, begging her to fix the stain on your blazer, and you just stood there innocently, like my sister had just brought home an angel."

My eyes begin to water. Suddenly I'm nervous a puddle is going to form underneath me, too. Sophie's clutching her mouth now, but I don't dare look at her. I'm sure she's choking back tears, but I can't bring myself to look.

"I think about it now, and that's the moment. That's when I fell for you. You were young, and so was I… That's why I put it down to being just a crush. But as we grew older, and I moved away for football… You never left. Not really, anyway."

"Train departing for London Central… Arriving at ten-twenty-four."

James' hands relax and mine fall back down by my side. He cups my cheek and the warmth of his palm against my skin makes me sink.

"What does this mean then?" I ask, directing my question at both James and Sophie.

"Well I-" Sophie goes to speak but she's cut off.

James throws his hand up at Sophie, snatching her words with a firm hand. Sophie ceases talking and rolls her eyes at her brother, turning her back on him with a childish poke of her tongue.

"Last night was the best night of my life," James begins, his arms are now wrapped tightly around my waist and he's so close I can see droplets of rain caught in his unshaven top lip. "We didn't *hook up*. No way. That was love, Victoria."

"What makes you so sure I feel the same as you do?" I ask.

"We belong together. The connection of our bodies last night, that's love, baby. I know you feel it, too. I just know it. Tell me you don't… Tell me you didn't feel that electricity between us."

We ignore the fake hurling Sophie is hunched over with beside us and she makes to walk off and finally give us this moment to ourselves. She finds a familiar face and begins pointing over at us, but I'm too involved with James to care.

"I felt it. Of course, I did…"

"I love you, Victoria. I always have loved you. I just never thought it would happen."

"I love you too, James."

James pulls me in to kiss him and the moment our lips touch, the train leaves the station, a symbolic moment that didn't pass me by.

"Oh, kiss her properly, for fucks sakes!" Sophie yells out across the platform.

Both laughing but refusing to cave to Sophie's demands, I link my hand in James', and we walk over to Sophie who is standing beside a tall guy who looks very familiar. His suit is well tailored, and his watch is golden and very, *very* nice.

"So, you've sorted him out then?" Sophie looks at me and smiles.

"I think so," I say, smiling as I look up to James, my hand firmly locked in his. "And you're OK with this?"

Sophie smiles, nods and as if we hadn't ever had a pact, turns her attention to the guy standing beside her.

"I'd like you guys to meet Diego…" Sophie looks up at the man who's skin is glowing with a brown tan that he definitely didn't obtain in Brighton this weekend. "He's here from Spain and we met a few nights ago."

Diego holds out his hand and offers a firm shake to James who looks down at his hand and laughs.

"Fuck off, bro!" James thumps his open palm against the curve of Diego's shoulder, sending him stumbling backwards. Sophie's eyes widen with shock, and I step back. "What are you doing down here, bro?"

"I did come down to check out this famous beach… But…" Diego looks down at Sophie and wiggles his brows, his heavy Spanish accent seemingly making her melt into the concrete landing. "I got distracted."

"You guys know each other?" Sophie's neck snaps and her eyes widen. She raises a brow to James and then flicks a shocked gaze across to Diego.

"Of course we do… He's 'keeper for the team, dumbass!"

James drops his hands back to mine and clasps firmly, leaving his sister behind as we walk back towards the exit of the station. Sophie and Diego linger somewhere behind us, but I'm in too much disbelief to care.

"So, what's for brunch?" James asks.

I lean up and peck a kiss on James' nose, smiling brightly with my eyes.

"How about we skip brunch and go straight for desert?" I tease.

"Oh, baby… You know how to please a man, don't you?"

Epilogue

James

"IT'S NOT TOO SOON!" I bark and the lads all shake their head at me. "You will understand one day. When you know she's the one, nothing else matters."

I tug at my wet laces and yank my cleats off my soaked socks. The changing room is filled with a subdued tiredness after an intense training session. We're getting ready for the game on the weekend and I'm nervous as fuck. We're playing Bristol City, who haven't been defeated all year. Their defence is tighter than a virgin nun on her wedding night and we've struggled for goals in the past three home games.

And on top of all that, Victoria will be in the stands, cheering me on for the first time since we officially started dating.

And on top of that, if all goes to plan, I'm proposing to her.

"So, you have already got the ring then?" Diego asks, his accent is thick, but his English is practiced enough that I'm able to understand him well.

I nod. "Yep."

Four of my teammates stare at me in disbelief. Diego is the only one who is smiling; Johnno, George and Tray are looking at me like I've got blood dripping from my eyes.

I didn't expect them to understand. They're younger than me, not by much, but I knew as well as most people that by the time you're over thirty years old, it's time to start getting your shit together. Or, at least, appear to be.

"I've wasted enough time, and I know she's perfect for me. That's all there is to it." I say, shooting up from the cold bench and grabbing my towel from my sports bag. "Now can I count on you to help me out? If this is going to work, we *have* to beat Bristol."

"You score the goals and I will keep a clean sheet to give us the best chance to win." Diego nods and turns to Johnno who looks bored.

"Yeah, fine. Whatever man. Your grave." Johnno grabs his towel and zooms across to the bathroom, letting the door slam behind him.

"Me and Tray think you're fucking looney, but fine. We're in."

George holds his fist out and I bump it with a smile stretching across my face. Diego slaps my ass as I pass him by. The lightest weight on my shoulders has been lifted. Now, there was just one huge, life changing weight remaining…

Will she say yes?

* * *

VICTORIA

"Oh my god!" I scream, my hands wildly slapping together in front of my face. My breath is visible in the freezing night air, a wave of steam flowing through the air with each excited round of applause I cheer out. "They smashed 'em! Smashed 'em!"

Sophie is just as bouncing beside me. She hasn't sat in her seat for the entirety of the two hours since the referee started the football match. We're right behind the goal at Hampstead FC's home ground, wild fans singing and chanting with huge grins across their frozen faces. James Hawkes has just kicked a hattrick to beat the previously undefeated Bristol City team.

James Hawkes.

My boyfriend.

Ever since we'd made it official, I still had to reinstate the fact that I was dating England's hottest footballing superstar. Several times a day I muttered under my breath that I was dating 'The Hawk'. Grant, my boss and horrible head chef at the restaurant, had yelled at me on more than one occasion about whispering to myself, demanding I speak up and communicate with the kitchen instead of to myself.

"Look! There's Diego! Oh, my goodness, he's simply…" Sophie clutched her hands over her chest, and even with the bone-chilling air burning her face, I could see her cheeks redden with a longing for her new 'friend'.

"A keeper?" I tease, nudging Sophie with my elbow.

"Oh, stop it! You know I'm not ready to settle down. I've too much to offer before that happens, girly," Sophie says, running a hand down her hips. "These curves aren't gonna tame themselves, baby."

I laugh, roll my eyes at my best friend and look down to the pitch. The team are doing a lap around the stadium, reaching up with their applause for the home fans who hadn't shut up since the whistle blew. Every touch of the ball was cheered loudly, and whenever Bristol tackled one of our players, boos echoed around the ground until we retrieved the ball again.

I squint and even from high up in the stands, I can see James at the back of the group of players. He's waving up at the stands as they turn at the corner flag, beginning their descent to our part of the stadium.

"He doesn't look very happy for someone who just scored a winning hat trick…" Sophie mutters beside me.

I nod. "No, he doesn't… He still looks nervous… He knows that game is over, right?"

Sophie laughs and my fingernails scrape against the palm of my hand inside my coat. Concern grips my thoughts, and a sinking feeling turns in my stomach. *I hope he's ok.* I had planned a 'Victory Night' at home for James which consisted of a nude massage in the sitting room. After a long rubdown, in which he would get as much from it as I would, I was to gift him an instantly redeemable ticket to do whatever he wanted to me in the bedroom.

The team work their way closer and I can't take my eyes off James. He's hovering at the back still, looking anywhere except up at me. I know he knows where we are in the stands, he got me the fucking tickets. Perhaps this is just how he is after a game? I mean, I've never been here directly after a match, so maybe this was normal?

I gulp down and a brutal blast of wind blows across me, making me grip my coat tighter. I see Diego on the pitch waving a few guys over to the advertisement board. They all pick it up and maneuverer it so it forms a walkway that leads from the pitch into the stands.

"What's he doing?" I ask, pointing to where Sophie was already staring at Diego with an unblinking stare.

"I don't know…" Sophie mumbles.

The team form two lines either side of the advertisement board. The coaches, players and assistants all line up facing each other, leaving a narrow space of green grass between the two lines of people as they face each other. They form a Guard of Honour that would look more at place down the road at Buckingham Palace, not on the edge of the frozen football pitch.

Everyone except James Hawkes is a part of it.

James is standing by himself in the centre of the two lines. His fingers are twisting nervously in his hand and the crowd around us settles down when the announcer's voice comes from the speakers in the roof above us.

"James Hawkes would like to invite his stunning girlfriend, Victoria, to join him at the edge of the field…"

My heart begins to race, and I forget how to breathe. I rub my ears which are now burning hot. Are they playing tricks on me? When Sophie gives me a push, a wide grin beaming from her face, I know they're not. I have no choice but to squeeze past the fans in our row and descend the steep steps of the grandstand.

I look up every few steps and see James at the bottom of the descent. He's still holding a straight face and I wonder what the fuck is going on. My legs are shaking and I have to concentrate on each step, if I fell down now, literally everyone in the stadium would see me because every single set of eyes is on me.

I reach the last step and James is there to take my hand, guiding me on to the soft green grass. It's wet and the heel of my boot sinks into the soft ground.

James leads the way, his football gear muddy and moist in the cold night air. His back is turned and all I can see of him is his wet hair, the name *HAWKES,* and a big number 10 on the back of his kit.

"James, what the hell is going on?" I whisper, and suddenly I realise that the stadium is silent.

My hand is sweaty in his, but when James turns and stops between the two lines of players and finally faces me, his face is stiff.

I gulp down.

"James…" I whisper again, nervously looking sideways at the team who all have their eyes on us. "Answer me, please…"

I'm begging now. This is torture and James isn't giving me anything. His eyes are barely blinking, his lips unmoving. I'm about to be exposed for something… humiliated… tortured… Something.

Whatever it is, I just wish he'd get it over with.

Out of the corner of my eye, I see the manager of the team tread silently over to James and hand him something in a small black box. I doubt whether I'm supposed to see him hand it to James, as he subtly breezes across the join the opposite line of players, but my senses are on high alert and right now, I'm aware of the kid in the front row who is jiggling his leg up and down in a squeaky seat.

"Victoria…"

James finally opens his mouth and it's like he's fired a cannonball and I'm just waiting for it to blow up in my face.

"You are the most beautiful girl I have ever met. I know we've only been seeing each other for a few weeks now, but I feel like I've known you my whole life." James is gripping both of my hands in his and my heart feels like it is going to burst out of my chest at any moment. "Your smile. Your sense of humour. Your incredible cooking… Oh my…"

There is a murmur of laughter that filters around us, but all of a sudden, I don't feel as exposed.

This isn't an attack.

I think I know what this is…

But, surely… surely not?

"But the best thing about you, is that you make me feel whole. You help me be a better person and I have found kindness inside of me that I didn't even know existed. You've completed me. And I want to make sure I remain the best possible person I can be for the rest of my life."

James drops to the wet grass, one knee sinking into the soil as he rests his hand on the other, popping open a ring box.

"Victoria, will you marry me?"

"James! Oh my god!" My hands clutch my mouth, and the feeling racing through my body is like nothing I have ever felt before. "James!"

I'm bouncing around and my head is turning to see wide smiles from all of his teammates. They're standing arm in arm now and one of the assistants is wiping a tear from her cheek.

"Ah… Victoria…" James says, pulling my focus back to him.

He looks panicked, and I realise I haven't answered him yet.

"Yes! Of course yes! Yes, yes, yes, yes… YES!"

James shoots up and kisses me. An applause, possibly the loudest of the night, rattles the tin on the roof of the stadium.

James pulls away for a second, slides the sparkling diamond ring over my finger and pulls me into his embrace again.

"I love you so much, Victoria," James says, his arms wrapped tightly around my waist.

"I love you, too. I'm going to be your wife!"

I bounce on the spot and hold my hand up to the grandstand. I show off the ring and I'm not sure if it's just me, but they cheer like I am part of the team.

And we have just won the best possible trophy in the world.

Thank you so much for reading BROKEN PROMISE!
This was Victoria and James' story - I hope you enjoyed the first in the series.

****

For a FREE SAMPLE of _Spanish Secret – Book Two,_ keep turning those pages!

Excerpt from next in series...

Spanish Secret – Curvy Girl Getaway Series

CHAPTER ONE

DIEGO SANCHEZ

"Catch you later on then, Big D?" Gary yells out, his head popping out from the black retractable roof on his red sportscar. "I need you on your game tonight, bro. You can wear that suit out, mate! There's plenty of fit girls in London needing a good Spanish tasting plate – if you know what I mean!"

"I said maybe, man," I yell back, smiling and waving a finger at my teammate. I tease him by pulling at my white suit blazer, winking.

I've been there and done that. I'm thirty-three years old. I'm OK with just going home and sitting on the couch. Falling asleep while watching TV, an empty bag of chips on the floor below me sounds like a fucking good Saturday night. But Gary McShane is young and wants to party whenever he's given the opportunity… Not me. Not anymore.

I wave at the assistants who are gathered in a meeting by the front door. I walk slowly through the front gates of Hampstead FC. The sky is fading into a hue of darker purple, the sun sinking low on the horizon. There's a brisk breeze that makes my entire body shiver and puts an extra hustle in my step.

Fucking freezing cold England.

I look over my shoulder and realize I'm the last player to leave the training ground. The Hampstead FC training ground is my second home, and the team have all made an effort to make me feel welcome ever since I arrived here from Valencia.

I was signed from the massive Spanish football team for a big fee six years ago. It was a record fee at the time: the most ever spent by a London club on an international goalkeeper. Instantly, I was under huge pressure because of my price tag. Pressure was something I was used to, though. Mother dearest had been piling that on me since I was old enough to talk.

But I worked hard and now I'm one of Spain's greatest exports to the British game. I haven't conceded a goal in four straight games and I'm favourite to take out the Golden Glove for the third year running.

Since my arrival, I've had many people inside the club help me out. Janine, the team masseuse, helped me get my apartment. Gary, who had now sped out of the car park at high speed, was kind enough to be always nagging me to go out with him, rounding up the 'lasses' and having our way with them. Gary was a nice man, British through and through. It was because of him that I had begged James 'The Hawk' Hawkes, our star striker and England's hottest prospect, to teach me some English slang.

In England, I quickly learned that a fish and chips shop was a 'chippy', and that if I wanted to settle my hangover with a bacon sandwich, the only way I wouldn't be laughed at by the pimpled teenager serving me early on a Sunday morning was to ask for a 'bacon sarni'.

The thought of a bacon sarni makes my stomach rumble, but the vibration of my phone pulls me quickly from that thought.

"Hello?" I answer without looking. I wave across at James Hawkes, my teammate, who is standing with his new fiancé and another girl whose face is covered by a scarf that's pulled up over her chin.

"Diego!" Mama's voice rattles my ear.

"Hola, Mama!" I say, surprise filling my voice. I click the button to unlock my Jeep and throw my bag on the passenger's seat before leaning back against the cold car. "How are you?"

Mama starts speaking quickly in Spanish, and I listen for a minute without taking in the words. My stomach melts at the sound of my native tongue. I miss Spain. My home. It's where I grew up.

But the reason I moved to England when I was twenty-eight is talking excitedly on the other end of the phone. We're one of the wealthiest families in our region, and my parents always put how we appeared to the outside world first, and my happiness and my own dreams and desires a very distant second.

The constant pressure from my parents, mainly Mama, to settle down and start a family, because you know… that's what all the other kids my age were doing. It came with the status of our family. It's a structured tier. It hasn't changed in centuries and that's that. No questions.

My desire to live my own life and not just fall in line was the biggest decision I ever made. I accepted the contract at Hampstead FC and I've never looked back. I was always one to fight the system, and much to Mama's disgust, I flew out within a week of the club's agreeing a fee for my services. I continued my single-man life without answering to the constant judgmental conversations every week. I broke free and the expectation to honour the system disappeared.

"Diego? Diego? Diego?!"

Mama hasn't changed. She still doesn't draw breath while she speaks. I hold the phone further away from my ear and it's still like she's on loudspeaker.

"Sorry, Ma," I say, speaking into the phone. "What did you say?"

"Papa… Me… coming visit," Mama says, and I'm impressed with her attempt at speaking English. "We… ah… at the airport now."

My eyes widen. Sparks explode in my chest and my knees give way.

"You're coming to England?"

"Si! Si!"

A smile lifts my cheeks; it's a nervous one. It's a smile filled with fear and hesitation. Memories of Mama's interrogations begin flooding my head. I can picture her arms flapping about in front of me, gold bracelets and rocks on every finger, waving wildly with each incorrect answer I give.

She's going to want to know everything… What am I eating? What am I studying? When did I last go for a checkup at the doctor? Am I cooking for myself? Why don't I get a personal chef?

Worst of all, and I can already hear the question like it's been burned into my brain: *Where is your girlfriend, Diego?*

"Oh, Mama! That's fantastic. Where are you staying?" I ask, feigning happiness as I begin pacing in the car park.

There's a pause, and I hear an announcement over a PA system. Papa mumbles something about first class passengers… Mama disagrees with him and they bicker for a moment. They're already at the airport.

Fuck. Fuck. Fuck!!!

My parents have left it until the last minute to surprise me. It's part of the plan. Mama's plan. They would have known for weeks they were planning to come to England. I spoke to Mama two weeks ago after the win over Bristol and there was no mention of it.

Just because they're rich, and barely have to work anymore, doesn't mean they have the magic ability to just drop everything in an instant.

No way. This is planned.

Mama wants to catch me off guard. I'm sure of it.

"Diego, we… uh… board now! Have bedroom ready!"

"Wait! Mama! Mama!"

The phone disconnects. All afternoon the manager had been grilling us, putting us through hard training drills and tiring exercises. Before that phone call, the last thing I felt like doing tonight was going to Soho to chat to random girls. Now, after hanging up the phone, I wanted to go with Gary McShane to some shady nightclub in a London side street and drink myself silly.

"Shit… Shit… Shit!" I slam my fist on my vehicle.

"You alright, mate?"

A voice from behind startles me and I spin quickly to see James frowning at me. The two girls he was with have joined him and they're all standing before me. Their brows are pulled together, and their hot breath surrounds our bodies with a heavy fog.

"Yeah," I huff. "I'm fine. It's just-"

I stop midsentence. There's a beautiful woman standing before me and I can't stop my eyes pulling up and down her body.

I'm breathless. I lose my train of thought.

We've met before…

Excitement races through me. With stunning blue eyes like hers, there's no way I would ever forget.

"Sophie…" I say, lifting her hand from her side and laying a soft peck on it. "How nice to see you. I didn't recognise you from across the lot. It must be all of these gorgeous layers you have on that disguised your beauty from me."

I watch her blush. The black scarf draped around her neck is pulled up over her face and hides the plush lips I remember wanting to latch on to. The beanie she's wearing is pulled right down below her ears. Her long dark hair is flowing around her shoulders, but her cute, puffy red cheeks can't hide.

I take her in. I've never seen anything as stunning as those blue eyes.

"We saw you pacing, mate," James says, and his hand clasps on my shoulder. "Are you sure you're ok?"

"Yeah, my parents have just decided to spring a surprise visit on me…" I say, training my eyes to stay fixed on James and not Sophie. "They're boarding a plane in Barcelona as we speak."

"Oh! Is this the famous *Mama* you're always talking about in the locker room?" James asks. He curls his arm around his fiancé, Victoria, pulls her in tightly. She snuggles in the crook of his shoulder, and I have to admit, even as someone who has never wanted to settle down, it looks nice to have a girl so comfortable in your arms.

"Si, that's her," I say, sneaking a glance to Sophie. Her lips have half a smile and she's hanging on every word. I look to her and smile. "What brings you to Hampstead, Miss Sophie?"

Sophie smiles and I swear she bats her lashes at me. I sneak a peek at her body and take in her stunning curves. Even with a coat pulled around her waist, it's so tight I can make out her large bust and wide hips. She's not like other women. She's got curves. She's more than a handful in all the right places. My cock twitches and I make sure to look back to her face to contain my excitement.

"I tagged along for the ride," Sophie says, her thick Londoner accent feeling as though it's floating across to me and kissing my ears. "Not much else going on, boring ol' life I lead…"

"Shame," I whisper, wishing my brain would operate properly so I could speak.

I can feel James looking from me to Sophie, and it's only then that I remember that he's her brother. I met Sophie in the club rooms a few weeks ago when she dropped in to see James who was taking off to Brighton for the weekend. Sophie was acting weird after James left, so we started talking and eventually I convinced Sophie to grab a quick cup of coffee. Despite my instant attraction, I got the impression that Sophie wasn't interested in a weird Spanish goalkeeper. I mean, if someone was staring at me with drool free-falling from their mouth, I wouldn't be too into it either.

"Is your Mom staying with you, Diego?" James asks as a gust of chilling wind sends a shiver right through me.

"I guess so," I say. "Who would know… The humungous city of London and all the money in the world and yet, they want to stay with me."

James laughs and his fiancé pops her face out from the warmth of his shoulder. "What's wrong with your ma, Diego?"

"Oh, nothing is *wrong* with her…" I sigh. "It's just normal parent behaviour. You know… *"Where is your life going, son?"* kind of stuff. And I really can't be bothered dealing with it this weekend. We finally have a weekend off, right James… No football. But now I would rather have footballs kicked at my face instead of being at home…"

They all laugh and my stomach flutters at the sound of Sophie's cute giggle. She covered her mouth when she laughed, and yet again, I swear she's fluttering those long, dark lashes at me. There's something different about this girl, something like I haven't felt before.

You're imagining it. Stop being a creep.

"Well, if we can help out at all… If you need saving you can call…" Victoria says.

"Thanks, I appreciate the offer," I smile. "It will be one very long weekend at my apartment explaining why I live in such a mess… And why I order Uber Eats every night… And why I still sleep alone… so I might just have to take you up on that offer."

I joke, hoping that I might get to hear that giggle again. Before Sophie's given the chance to bless my ears, James jumps across in front of me, his eyes wide. The girls are forced to take a giant step backwards to make way for James' who's bouncing body is shooting up and down with excitement.

"I know! I've got it!" James' eyes are huge and he's not blinking. "Sophie can be your girlfriend! That would keep them at bay!"

"What?" Victoria cries out from behind James.

"Ummmm… What?" Sophie mimics Victoria, and my brows are halfway up my face, too.

"Yeah! It's just like in the movies!" James circles to his fiancé. "You fake a relationship to cover up your boring life." He turns back to me and shrugs. "No offence, mate."

"None taken," I shrug.

"It's simple really…" James continues. "Sophie stays with you for the weekend, you hang out, have a drink with the parents and a nice meal. Take them out sightseeing or some shit on Saturday and before you know it, BAM!" James throws his hands up in the air and his mouth is a wide grin. "They've gone home, you can just return to how you were living before. All is good again!"

"Oh, please," Sophie pipes up and is now crossing her arms over her chest. "I wouldn't help cover up a single thing. If anything, I would cause more issues than I would help solve. Right, Diego?"

I'm looking from James to Sophie and then to Victoria. They're all staring back at me. On one hand, I think it's stupid and my parents would never fall for it.

But then, on the other hand, I would get to spend all weekend with Sophie…

"Well, it's not the worst idea I've ever heard…" I say softly, looking through the tops of my eyes, gauging Sophie's reaction.

"Yes!" James jumps up again, making everyone scuttle backwards another few feet. "Come on, Soph! Help the guy out!"

Sophie sucks in a deep breath and presses her hands to her hips. "And you really want me to be your fake girlfriend?"

"It might be fun," I say. "But the choice is yours."

I'm not sure what it is about Sophie that has me obsessed with making sure she's by my side. I've never been interested in a relationship before. I mean, that's what's got me in to this situation to begin with. There's something about this girl, though… She's different.

Please say yes…

"OK," Sophie breaths and my heart leaps. "OK, I'm in."

GET THIS BOOK ON AMAZON TODAY!

MORE BOOKS BY C.H. JAMES?
Yes, please!

Instalove Short Reads:

Curvy Girl Getaway - A British Soccer Romance Series

Broken Promise – Book One

Spanish Secret – Book Two

Kiss at Midnight – Book Three

Rebound Suite – Book Four

Curvy Girl Getaway Series BOXSET

Curvy Kilts - A Scottish Highland Romance Series

ANDREW – My First Love – Book One

ROBERT – My Older Man – Book Two

The Locker Room Series - A Steamy Hockey Romance Series

My Curvy Puck – Book One

Captain's Curvy Puck – Book Two

Puck My Roommate – Book Three

My Virgin Puck – Book Four

Operation: Curvy - A Military Navy SEAL Romance Series

Sealing Her Fate – Book One

Operation Seal Her – Book Two

Surrender To Her – Book Three

Her Curvy Explosion – Book Four

Falls Creek Falcons – A Bad Boy Hockey Romance Series

Bad Boys: Shut Out

Bad Boys: Game Over

Bad Boys: Pressure

Bad Boys: Hard Play

Mountain Men of Falls Creek – A Wild Alpha Man Romance Series

Curvy Cabin

Curvy Camper

Curvy Christmas Collection – A Steamy Holiday Romance Series

Santa's Sack

Billionaire's Naughty Elf

Full Length Novels:

HATE The Game – Oaks East Vipers - Book One

HATE The Player – Oaks East Vipers – Book Two

About the Author

www.ingramcontent.com/pod-product-compliance
Lightning Source LLC
Chambersburg PA
CBHW052143150726
48002CB00003B/1051